Dedication

For Samuel,

Who always sees the silver lining.

-E.S.N.

Text Copyright 2001 by Elizabeth Sussman Nassau
Illustrations Copyright 2001 Margot Janet Ott

Published by Health Press
P.O. Box 37470
Albuquerque, NM 87176
505-888-1394
www.healthpress.com

Foreword

Approximately 1.5 million Americans have peanut allergy and the number seems to be increasing. Peanut allergy is the most common cause of food-induced anaphylactic reactions in the U.S. and is responsible for over 10,000 visits to hospital emergency rooms each year. Unlike other forms of food allergy, most children with peanut allergy will not outgrow their allergy to peanuts. Scientists are trying to determine why peanut allergy seems to be increasing and why peanuts tend to cause more severe reactions. Happily, clinical trials have begun to test new therapies to treat peanut allergy and vaccine that may "cure" peanut allergy are under investigation.

In the meantime, education of patients, families, and caregivers remains the key. *The Peanut Butter Jam* is a wonderful story that provides great insight into what it is like to live with a peanut allergy. Sam's day at school is reminiscent of what hundreds of peanut allergic children face each day. It provides a life-like account of what can happen during an anaphylactic reaction to peanut and how a well-prepared school should respond. Elizabeth Sussman Nassau obviously has "been there" and in *The Peanut Butter Jam* has provided an entertaining story for children and educational primer for adults. It is a must read for families with food allergic children and educators with food allergic students.

Hugh A. Sampson, M.D.
Professor of Pediatrics & Biomedical Sciences
Mount Sinai School of Medicine

*I*t should have been a typical day in Mr. Maglio's class.

The class had just begun working on their nature project – bird feeders. It looked like fun. First you took an ice-cream cone. Then you rolled it in peanut butter and after that, in birdseed. Finally, you strung a shoelace through and – *voila!* – a bird feeder. But the project had been a disaster for Sam.

That's because Sam was allergic to peanuts. He was so allergic that he couldn't even sit near his friends when they ate peanut butter sandwiches for lunch. Because of his allergy, Sam couldn't make a bird feeder.

Instead, he sat at Mr. Maglio's desk, pouring birdseed and counting laces.

Jack had teased him. "What's the matter, Sam-u-el?" he called in a sing-song voice, licking his sticky fingers. "Afraid of a little jar of peanut butter?" Sam tried to ignore Jack. But he was sick of peanut jokes, sick of kids who shoved their peanut snacks in his face, sick of being different.

Sam wanted to show Jack that he wasn't afraid. After all, it *had* been a long time since he had seen Dr. Greene, the allergist. He rarely needed the allergy syrup that tasted like cough medicine. And he had *never* needed the emergency shot of epinephrine that he always carried in his backpack. Sam thought for a long minute. Then, with a sinking feeling in his stomach, he stood up.

Sam walked straight to Jack's table. He picked up an ice-cream cone. Carefully, he rolled it in peanut butter. No reaction. Slowly, neatly, he covered it with birdseed. Still no problem. Sam was about to give Jack a "thumbs-up" when he heard Mr. Maglio shout, "Sam! What are you thinking? Let's MOVE! Wash your hands <u>right now</u>!"

Sam's smile faded. "Okay," he muttered, walking to the sink at the back of the room. He stopped to brush away an eyelash. As he washed, Sam's eyes began to itch. Then both eyes began to throb. Suddenly, his cheeks felt hot. Sam glanced up to see Jack staring at him. "Sam," Jack whispered, "your face is blowing up."

Sam started to speak, but a funny cough came out instead. As he looked around, he realized that his classmates had stopped their work to look at him. Mr. Maglio murmured something to the class aide before announcing calmly, "Sam and I are going to the nurse's office." He grabbed Sam's backpack and raced down the hall with Sam in tow.

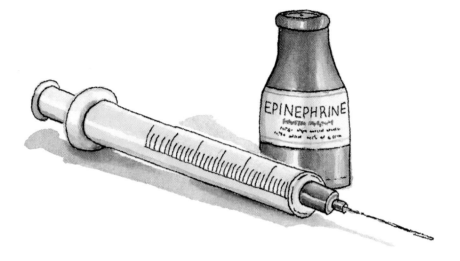

The nurse knew what to do. With one hand, she pushed up his shorts. With the other, she injected his emergency medicine into his thigh. *Ouch!* Sam thought. *That hurts*. But a few moments later, he was breathing more easily.

When Sam stopped coughing, the nurse gave him syrup to drink. By that time, an ambulance had arrived. Sam had never ridden in one before and he didn't want to ride in one now. He was relieved when Mr. Maglio came along.

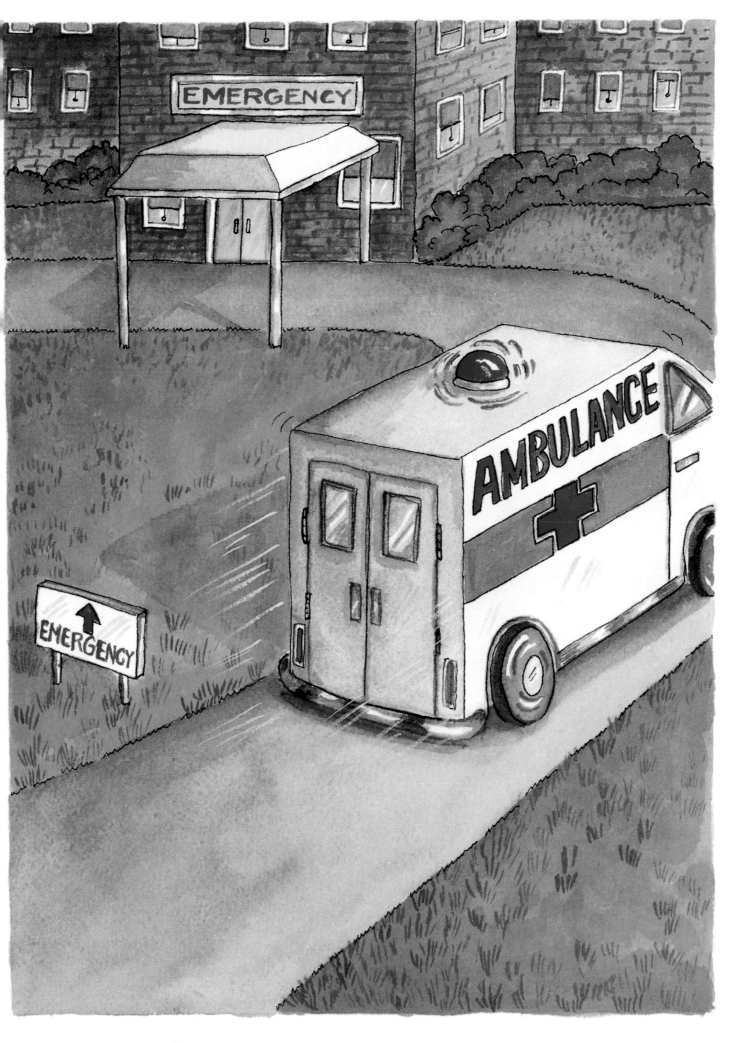

In no time at all, they were at the hospital. Sam was alarmed. Wasn't the Emergency Room for broken arms and car accidents? Was he *that* sick?

By the time his mother rushed in, Sam was so glad to see her that he didn't complain when she hugged him and stroked his hair. She thanked Mr. Maglio, who squeezed Sam's shoulder. "See you in school, buddy," he said as he left.

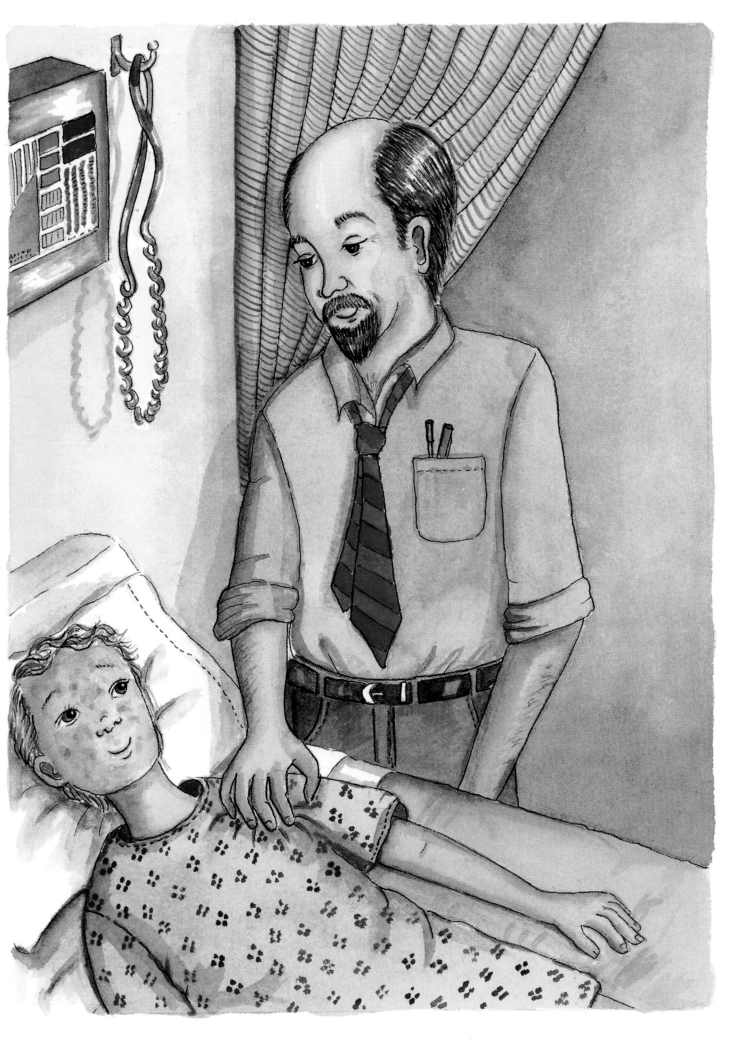

Sam jumped as the curtain opened and a tall woman with big glasses and red hair entered the cubicle. "Hi, Sam," said Dr. Greene. "Your principal just called. I hear you've had an exciting day."

Dr. Greene examined Sam thoroughly. She checked his heart rate. She listened to him breathe, her metal stethoscope cold on his back and chest. She looked in his eyes, nose, mouth. Then she looked <u>into</u> his eyes and asked what had happened.

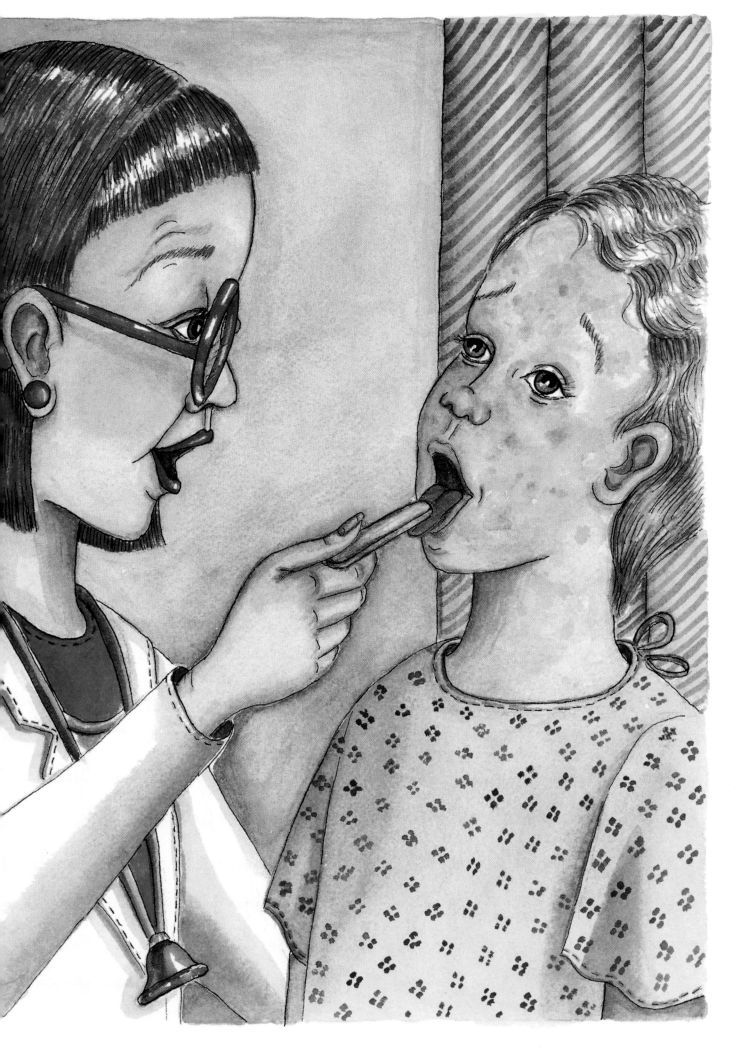

Sam explained about Jack, the bird feeders, the teasing at school. He was sorry he had frightened his mother and worried his teacher, not to mention his classmates. Dr. Greene didn't seem concerned about that. "Sam," she said gently, "you risked your life on a dare. Now be honest: was it worth the risk?"

Sam began to cry. He was frightened and angry all at once. Dr. Greene spent a long time talking with Sam and his mother. They discussed what to do when someone teased him or offered him unwrapped food. They talked about feeling different. Dr. Greene said she had hated wearing glasses in the first grade. "I was the only one," she remembered.

Then Dr. Greene told them about a kid's group where Sam could meet other children with allergies. She wrote down the telephone number and handed it to him. Sam and his mother left the hospital with a plan.

The next day, Sam was back in school. In class, he told Mr. Maglio about the allergy group he would soon attend. At lunch, he told his friends about a medical "alert" bracelet his mother had ordered for him. At recess, Jack told Sam he was sorry for teasing him about the peanut butter.

"That's okay, Jack," said Sam. "I was wrong, too."

After school, Sam invited Jack to his house.

"I'm not sure," Jack said, "Do you have pets?"

"No," replied Sam, "why?"

"Well," Jack answered, suddenly shy. "I guess I forgot to tell you –
I'm allergic to cats."

Sam smiled at his new friend. They had more in common than he had
known.

The two boys laughed as they headed for home.